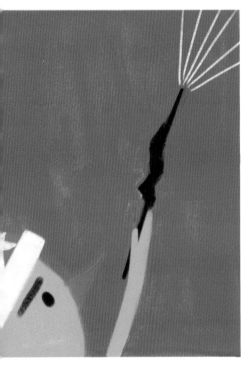
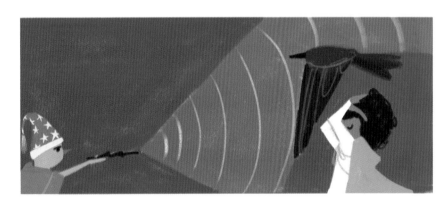

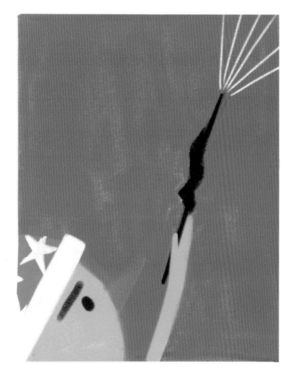
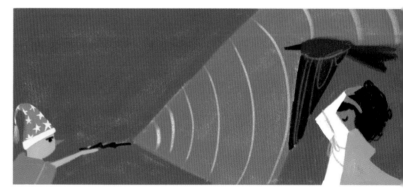

FALALAHHHH

Brilliant Bea

by Shaina Rudolph and Mary Vukadinovich
illustrated by Fiona Lee

Magination Press • Washington, DC • American Psychological Association

To my Harlie—never dull your sparkle—*SR*

For my mom, who was my first story teller.
For Millicent and Otto, my favorite story
tellers. And for all my students past and
present, you inspired Bea—*MV*

To all the good teachers in my life—your
impact is boundless—*FL*

Books for Kids From the
American Psychological Association

maginationpress.org

Magination Press is a registered trademark of the American Psychological Association. Order books at maginationpress.org, or call 1-800-374-2721.

Book design by Rachel Ross
Typeset in EasyReading

 Font **DYSLEXIA FRIENDLY**

High-legibility typeface

Printed by Phoenix Color, Hagerstown, MD

Library of Congress Cataloging-in-Publication Data
Names: Rudolph, Shaina, author. | Vukadinovich, Mary, author. | Lee, Fiona (Illustrator), illustrator.
Title: Brilliant Bea/by Shaina Rudolph and Mary Vukadinovich; illustrated by Fiona Lee.
Description: Washington, D.C.: Magination Press, [2021] | Summary: With help from Ms. Bloom and some new friends, Beatrice discovers that learning differently is not something to be afraid of, and that dyslexia does not define who she is.
Identifiers: LCCN 2020054857 (print) | LCCN 2020054858 (ebook) | ISBN 9781433837418 (hardcover) | ISBN 9781433837425 (ebook)
Subjects: CYAC: Dyslexia—Fiction. | Schools--Fiction. | Storytelling—Fiction.
Classification: LCC PZ7.1.R83 Bri 2021 (print) | LCC PZ7.1.R83 (ebook) | DDC [E]—dc23
LC record available at https://lccn.loc.gov/2020054857

Manufactured in the United States of America
10 9 8 7 6 5 4 3 2 1

They say your imagination can take you anywhere.
I remember when mine didn't let me leave the classroom.

While the rest of the kids in Room 11 were lined up for recess, I was stuck finishing my work again.

I was stucker than stuck.

Stuck in Stucksville,

population: 1.

Mom always said I have a way with words.

Dad always said I'm a real word slinger.

My little brother Charlie always said I'm the greatest storyteller on Earth.

The thing is, though, reading and writing are extra hard for me. Mom and Dad told me that's called dyslexia. It's like the words jump around the page and my eyes try to shoot laser beams to catch them.

Every day at school I was the last one done with my work, the daydreamer staring out the window, and the one Ms. Bloom had to use up all of her patience on.

I would usually try to tell her a real doozy of a story to get her off topic.

It didn't make me very popular with the other kids.

Whenever I had to read out loud in class, I just wanted to melt in my chair like a popsicle on a hot day.

If it was Hidden Ham Surprise day in the cafeteria, I could sometimes fool Ms. Bloom that I needed to see Nurse Leo.

If I did have to read, it sounded like I was reading in slow motion and fast-forward at the same time.

Writing wasn't much better. It's like my pencil wouldn't write what my brain is thinking.

"Beatrice, what's the hiccup? Can I read what you have so far?"
Ms. Bloom asked. I nodded. She looked at the words I had on
the page:

"I woent let dullying bring me doun."
"What is dullying?" Ms. Bloom asked.
"Bullying, not dullying!" I pronounced.

In her most kind way, Ms. Bloom said, "I think you've figured it out
with your brilliant brain, Beatrice. Bullying is dull!"

"Do you know what brilliant means?" Ms. Bloom asked.

"It means super smart," I answered in a super smart way.

"It means bright and radiant, Beatrice. That's the opposite of dull."

I'm

BRILLIANT!

The next day, Ms. Bloom kept me after school. My heart hop-scotched its way to her desk. She opened her drawer and pulled out some sort of ancient device.

"This is for you to tell your stories to. It's a tape recorder. Push this button here and away you go."

"Uh, thanks Ms. Bloom. I will take good care of it."

Sitting alone at recess was not a new activity for me, but this time I pushed the red button, cleared the frogs from my throat, and let the words flow.

"It all began one ordinary day...and in the end, the three misfits knew they had experienced something extraordinary."

"Why are you talking to yourself and what is the weird thing around your neck, Beatrice?" asked Rudy. Normally I would shrivel up and just wish him away. Not today.

"It records all of my stories," I answered snappily.

"...so the small but mighty girl with the scarlet cape and the golden griffin went into the Cave of Enchantment, where they found the nightingale whose magic could restore her voice."

"I love to draw. Maybe I can make some pictures for your stories."

"I'd like that." I smiled back. "You can call me Bea. That's what my friends call me."

That afternoon, Rudy helped me feel unstuck.

After a little time, recess meant that me and
my new friends gathered by the oak tree
and sailed off to far away adventures...

"...then the wizard pointed his staff at the girl, but the nightingale spread its wings over the girl to let the light shine down on her. The whole cave glowed as the girl's voice came back to her. It rose until its beauty shrunk the wizard to the size of a goosebump."

...or just a game of Four Square.

Learning differently wasn't something to be afraid of anymore, either.

My best friend and I created a comic book that the class loved so much, Ms. Bloom made copies for everyone to take home.

And someday, you will become who you were meant to be.

Reader's Note
by Ellen B. Braaten, PhD

Brilliant Bea provides readers with an insightful glimpse into the emotional journey and experiences of a young, creative, and yes, *brilliant* young reader, named Bea, with dyslexia. Bea helps the reader understand the typical challenges experienced at school. She is by her own words, "stuck." Reading aloud is difficult and embarrassing for her. She often displays behaviors, such as asking to see the school nurse, as a way of "getting out" of reading and writing activities or instruction. She describes her reading as a mix of slow motion and fast-forward and says that the words "jump around the page."

The book also provides insight into what can help kids with dyslexia feel more empowered. Bea not only shares her struggles, she also shows the resiliency often displayed by children with dyslexia and other learning differences. Bea is a bubbly and engaged learner who has a lot to say. In the hands of a skilled teacher, who defines her as "brilliant"—a "bright and radiant" student—she finds a way to express herself through using a tape recorder to compose her thoughts. This is an example of an appropriate accommodation for kids with dyslexia who have trouble expressing their thoughts through written expression. When appropriately accommodated, students feel confident of their ability to be successful and this can result in better experiences outside of the classroom, as shown in Bea's new friendship with Rudy.

This book is a wonderful way to open up a conversation with a child with dyslexia, or to expose children without dyslexia to the concept of learning differences and challenges. It also shows how children can be supportive of other learners and learning styles. You can ask questions such as:

- "How do you think Bea feels when her imagination is going wild with ideas?"
- "How does she feel when everyone else is lining up for recess?"
- "What about Rudy? What is he doing to support his friend? How do you think this makes him feel?"

WHAT IS DYSLEXIA?

Children with dyslexia have difficulty accurately and fluently reading words. A few decades of research have shown that *phonological processing* is the specific problem that underlies dyslexia. Phonological processing is another way of saying *phonics skills*—the skills involved in understanding the rules by which sounds go with letters or letter groupings. For instance, children must learn that cat has three sounds (also called *phonemes*) in it: *c – a – t*. When the "a" in "cat" is changed to "u" (a different phoneme, or sound), the word changes to "cut." In order to do this, children have to be able to hear and segment these sounds. Then, they have to blend the sounds together to form the word. Children with dyslexia have difficulty perceiving the individual sounds in words, and therefore have trouble with the task of breaking words down to sound them out for reading or spelling.

Many parents and caregivers think that the definition of dyslexia means that children reverse letters or write backwards. While some children with dyslexia *do* tend to reverse letters, this is not the defining feature. Instead, children with dyslexia have difficulty learning phonics and have trouble reading fluently—that is, at a normal speed without errors. It is a struggle for them to sound out words they have not seen before and spelling can be quite difficult. Although some children with dyslexia dislike reading, some actually do like to read and a fair number of children with dyslexia can have good reading comprehension strategies even though they haven't read every word accurately.

WHAT MIGHT SYMPTOMS OF DYSLEXIA LOOK LIKE IN YOUNG CHILDREN?

Children with dyslexia do not have an event in their past, like an accident, that caused dyslexia and for the most part, their early development is normal. However, some children show problems pronouncing words (sometimes called *articulation* problems) or speech delays in early childhood. By first or second grade, they typically show problems learning to read. In fact, problems might be evident as early as kindergarten in that they may have difficulty learning the alphabet or letter sounds. Dyslexia has a strong genetic component and tends to run in families. Because dyslexia is a language-based learning difference, many children with dyslexia have difficulties, sometimes subtle, with other aspects of language, such as verbal memory, word finding (finding the right word at the right time), and organizing their thoughts. Problems with early writing skills, such as writing letters, are quite common as well.

HOW CAN I FIND OUT IF MY CHILD HAS DYSLEXIA?

An evaluation for dyslexia is typically provided by a psychologist, who completes a test battery tailored to a child's age and level of education. The evaluation can be completed through your local school system or from a licensed psychologist or educational professional. The evaluation needs to establish that there is a reading problem by evaluating reading decoding, phonetic processing, spelling, and comprehension skills. A comprehensive evaluation will also typically include a measure of intellectual or problem-solving abilities, measures of general language functioning, and other academic areas. It is important to note that there is no single test that can provide a diagnosis of dyslexia. The diagnosis can only be made after a comprehensive battery of tests have been completed. It is the overall pattern that is important, which can look very different depending on the child.

WHAT ARE THE TREATMENTS FOR DYSLEXIA?

Two areas are important in treating and coping with dyslexia: *remediation* and *accommodation*. *Remediation* is about helping kids get the skills they need to be competent readers. There are fortunately a number of proven reading methods for teaching children with dyslexia how to read and they all have a few things in common. They are *multisensory* in the approach (using many senses, such as visual cues, touch, verbal skills). They are *sequential* in that each skill builds on another one. And they are *phonologically based* (they use phonics to teach reading). Some of the more popular approaches are the Orton-Gillingham, Wilson Reading System, and Lindamood Bell. While each of these programs emphasizes slightly different aspects of reading, research has indicated that each of these methods are as good as the other as long as they are implemented by well-trained tutors frequently enough to make a difference and for a sufficient duration (in other words, not stopping tutoring before a child has mastered the concepts).

Bea's teacher, Ms. Bloom, understood the importance of *accommodations*. These are the supports that are used to help children while they are learning to read and spell. They are also used for older learners. Using voice recognition software for writing, listening to books on tape, and having extra time on tests are some of the most helpful accommodations.

If you are concerned about your child's reading skills, a good first step is to talk to your child's teacher. If more information is needed, child psychologists can provide support and additional testing. With appropriate remediation and accommodations, the vast majority of children with dyslexia can learn to read quite well and become successful adults—even writing their own books, just like Bea.

Ellen B. Braaten, PhD, is the executive director of the Learning and Emotional Assessment Program (LEAP) at Massachusetts General Hospital and associate professor of psychology at Harvard Medical School. She is also the coauthor of *Straight Talk about Psychological Testing for Kids* and *Bright Kids Who Can't Keep Up.*

Shaina Rudolph is an author and educator in the Los Angeles area. She has worked alongside students with unique learning needs for the last 10 years. Shaina also co-authored *All My Stripes: A Story For Children With Autism*. Visit @ShainaRudolph_ on Instagram.

Mary Vukadinovich has been working with students with language-based differences for the last 16 years. As a learning specialist in Los Angeles, Mary values the opportunity to teach diverse learners, including students with dyslexia. Mary believes all her students can be successful, and she is constantly inspired by how brightly they shine. Visit @Mary_Vukadinovich on Instragram.

Fiona Lee is a children's book illustrator living in central Vermont. Her background in education and science illustration informs how she approaches all of her illustration projects today. Visit fionaleestudios.com, @Fiona_LeeStudio on Twitter, and @FionaLee_Draws on Instagram.

Magination Press is the children's book imprint of the American Psychological Association. APA works to advance psychology as a science and profession and as a means of promoting health and human welfare. Magination Press books reach young readers and their parents and caregivers to make navigating life's challenges a little easier. It's the combined power of psychology and literature that makes a Magination Press book special. Visit maginationpress.org, and @MaginationPress on Facebook, Twitter, Instagram, and Pinterest.

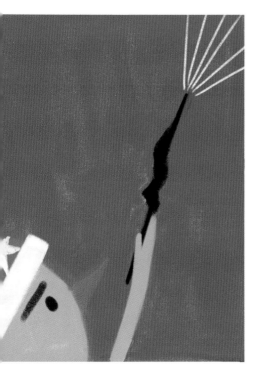
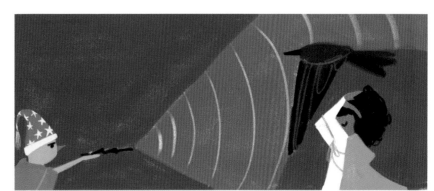

FALALAHHHH

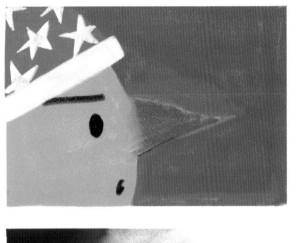

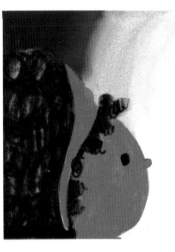
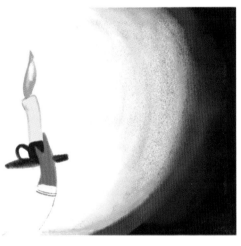